The Great Dinosaur Hunt

A WOODLAND MYSTERY

By Irene Schultz

To my dad, Papa Moe, who passed on his love
of reading to his children

The Great Dinosaur Hunt
©1996 Wright Group Publishing, Inc.
©1996 Story by Irene Schultz
Cover and cameo illustrations by Taylor Bruce
Interior illustrations by Meredith Yasui
Map illustration by Alicia Kramer

Woodland Mysteries™
© Wright Group Publishing, Inc.

The Woodland Mysteries were created by the
Wright Group development team.

The Wright Group
19201 120th Avenue NE
Bothell, WA 98011

Printed in the United States of America

10 9 8 7 6 5 4 3

ISBN: 0-7802-7230-7

What family solves mysteries...has adventures all over the world...and loves oatmeal cookies?

It's the Woodlanders!

Sammy Westburg (10 years old)
His sister Kathy Westburg (13)
His brother Bill Westburg (14)
His best friend Dave Briggs (16)
His best grown-up friend Mrs. Tandy
And Mop, their little dog!

The children all lost their parents, but with Mrs. Tandy have made their own family.

Why are they called the Woodlanders? Because they live in a big house in the Bluff Lake woods. On Woodland Street!

Together they find fun, mystery, and adventure. What are they up to now?

Read on!

Meet the Woodlanders!

Sammy Westburg

Sammy is a ten-year-old wonder! He's big for his fifth-grade class, and big-mouthed, too. He has wild hair and makes awful spider faces. Even so, you can't help liking him.

Bill Westburg

Bill, fourteen, is friendly and strong, and only one inch taller than his brother Sammy. He loves Sammy, but pokes him to make him be quiet! He's in junior high.

Kathy Westburg

Kathy, thirteen, is small, shy, and smart. She wants to be a doctor some day! She loves to be with Dave, and her brothers kid her about it. She's in junior high, too.

Dave Briggs
Dave, sixteen, is tall and blond. He can't walk, so he uses a wheelchair and drives a special car. He likes coaching high-school sports, solving mysteries, and reading. And Kathy!

Mrs. Tandy
Sometimes the kids call her Mrs. T. She's Becky Tandy, their tall, thin, caring friend. She's always ready for a new adventure, and for making cookies!

Mop
Mop is the family's little tan dog. Sometimes they have to leave him behind with friends. But he'd much rather be running after Sammy.

Table of Contents

Chapter 1:
The Horned Toad

It was late afternoon.

The five members of the Woodland family stopped their van on a little road in Arizona.

Fourteen-year-old Bill Westburg got out. He looked down at the wide, brick-colored canyon.

The wild land reached as far as he could see.

He said, "I can't believe we finally made it!"

Sammy, Bill's ten-year-old brother, jumped out of the van after him.

He began walking in circles on the dry rocky ground.

He said, "Well? Where are all the dinosaur bones? Where are the fossils Dr. Luke told us about? All I see are plain old rocks!"

His thirteen-year-old sister Kathy laughed as she hopped out of the van.

She handed Sammy a pick and a hammer. She said, "Here, Sammy. Start digging for them!"

Mrs. Tandy took a wheelchair out of

the back.   She carried it over to the driver's side of the van.

She said, "Here's your chair, Dave!"

Dave Briggs, sixteen, lowered his body into it from the driver's seat.

Then he took hold of his legs.   He lifted his feet one at a time to the wheelchair's footrests.

He said, "Thanks, Mrs. T.   Wow, it's sure hot!   We better get the tent set up in some shade!"

He and Mrs. Tandy started helping Bill and Kathy un-load ...

flashlights
boots
coats
pots and pans
sleeping bags
... and bottles of water.

Sammy was still walking around in circles. Suddenly he dropped the pick and hammer.

He said, "What's wrong with you guys? Don't you know you should unload the important things first? The FOOD!"

He pulled out two large boxes full of food. He put one on top of the other.

Then he picked up both boxes at once.

Bill ran over to him. He said, "Sammy! That's way too much for you to carry!"

He tried to take the top box.

Sammy said, "I can carry them both. Easy. I'm stronger than you!"

Then ... he tripped.

The top box fell.

Food flew out all around.

Sammy said, "Now see what you made me do!"

He slammed into Bill's side. He slipped, and fell with the bottom box.

Now he was mad!

He looked wild!

He jumped up.

He made his hands into fists.

He made his bull-dog face.

He looked ready to hit Bill.

But Bill made a sudden jump toward something on the ground.

He yelled, "Got it!"

Sammy said, "What? Got what?"

Bill kept his hands closed. He said, "Why should I show this to a kid who's going to hit me?"

He turned his back to Sammy. He began to talk to the thing in his hands. "Where did you come from, little fellow?"

Sammy said, "Come on, Bill. Let me see. I'm not going to hit you. I was just kidding."

Bill said, "OK, then. LOOK!"

He opened his hands.

There sat a little lizard-like animal.

But it was fat, like a toad.

It had two little horns on the back of its head.

It was a dusty red-brown color, just

the color of the ground.

It had scales all over it, and saw-like bumps on its head and down its back and tail.

Sammy leaned way down and took a close look, almost nose-to-nose.

The animal looked right at him.

Then, SQUIRT!

Two thin jets of blood shot out of its eyes!

They hit Sammy right in the face.

Sammy yelled, "HEY! I've been shot!"

Chapter 2:
A Stranger in the Night

Mrs. Tandy, Kathy, and Dave hurried over.

Mrs. Tandy saw a tiny bit of blood on Sammy's head.

She cried, "Oh, my! Here, Sammy."

She handed him a tissue. "Are you OK?"

Sammy said, "Sure! That's not MY blood. That stupid little horned rat got me right between the eyes! What a sharpshooter!"

Kathy said, "That's what we can call him! Sharpshooter."

Sammy said, "You know, he looks sort of like a dinosaur. Like some I saw in a book at school. I even remember the names."

He pronounced the words carefully. "A Tri-cer-a-tops. And a Steg-o-saur-us."

Bill said, "How come you can remember that, but you can't remember when it's your turn to dry the dishes!"

Dave laughed. He said, "Well, you're not far off, Sammy. This little guy is a distant cousin of the dinosaurs."

Sammy said, "You're kidding! Come on. All the dinosaurs died millions of years ago!"

Dave nodded. "I know. But dinosaurs were reptiles, and this is a reptile, too.

"It's really a lizard. But it's called a horned toad because of its fat little toad shape.

"I read somewhere that they squirt blood from their eyes to scare their enemies."

Sammy said, "I wish I could squirt blood out of my eyes ... and all over Bill!"

11

Bill pretended he didn't hear him. He said, "Dave, did you read about what these guys eat? Tacos? Hot dogs? Bugs?"

Dave said, "A lot of lizards eat insects and spiders. Sharpshooter probably does, too."

Kathy said, "Yuck! Glad I'm not a lizard."

Bill said, "I think I'll keep him. Just for tonight. Maybe for now I'll just put him in a paper bag. I can figure out a cage later.

"Let's pick up all this food and go set up our tent."

Sammy said, "OK, Bill. And I'll help you make a cage for him.

"Then tomorrow morning we can let him out and watch him find his buggy breakfast."

Bill and Dave pulled the huge tent out of the van.

Dave said, "Lay it on the arms of my chair, Bill. I'll carry it."

He pointed to a spot down in the canyon. He said, "Let's set up there."

Kathy said, "Perfect. The canyon walls should keep the sun off of it most of the day."

Mrs. Tandy said, "And the river's only thirty feet away!"

Bill said, "And there's plenty of room for Dr. Luke's tent when he gets here tomorrow."

They made their bumpy way down into the canyon.

Pretty soon the tent was set up ... and they finished carrying everything down from the van.

Sammy said, "Good grief. We've got enough stuff here to start a hotel!"

They found some dead branches and built a fire to roast hot dogs for dinner.

They used their camp stove to heat water for soup.

Sammy mixed up some water and powdered milk. He added a few drops of vanilla and some sugar.

He said, "Usually I HATE dried milk, but I love it this way."

They sat down on the ground and ate. After dinner, Kathy, Dave, and Mrs. Tandy carefully put their paper plates and napkins in the fire.

Sammy and Bill worked on the cage.

First Bill put Sharpshooter on the ground.

He put a little pan of water near him. Then he put a cardboard box upside-down over him.

Sammy poked air holes in the box.

And last, Bill put a stone on top of it, so it wouldn't blow away.

Then the Woodlanders went to their

tent to sleep.

In the morning Bill was the first one out of his sleeping bag.

He whispered in Sammy's ear, "Come on, let's go look at Sharpshooter."

The two boys sneaked out of the tent on their hands and knees in their underwear.

Then they walked to the side of the tent where they had left the horned toad.

The box was tipped on its side.

15

Sharpshooter was gone!

Sammy said, "Wow, I never thought that little guy was strong enough to knock the box over.

"That rock we put on top was HEAVY!"

Bill said, "He couldn't have done it. Maybe some big animal came by in the night."

By then Kathy had sneaked out of the tent.

She said, "Hey, why don't you two put on some pants! Are you going to carry that horned toad around Arizona in your underwear?"

Bill said, "We aren't going anywhere with him. Sharpshooter's gone. Something tipped over his box."

Kathy looked at the box. She said, "Oh, I'm so sorry."

Then she looked scared.

16

She said, "That must have been the noise I heard in the middle of the night. Footsteps right near my head, outside the tent.

"I thought one of you had gotten up, so I just went back to sleep."

Bill said, "I didn't get up last night."

Sammy said, "Me, either."

Dave and Mrs. Tandy came over to them.

Mrs. Tandy said, "What's all the fuss?"

When they told her, she said, "Well, don't worry too much about any big animal. Justin said we didn't have to be afraid of the wild life here.

"I remember talking about it when he asked us to help him."

Dave said, "That's right. Dr. Luke only mentioned antelope. And deer. And I think foxes."

Mrs. Tandy said, "Well, I hope that's

17

true! We want to help Justin get this piece of land set aside as a national park. But we don't want to let some animal get us."

Kathy said, "Maybe ... if we look around ... we could find out what kind of animal it was."

Dave said, "Good idea. Spread out, guys. Maybe we can find some droppings. Or some fur. Or some tracks."

The next minute Dave yelled, "Hey, I found something!"

They all ran over to him.

He said, "I know what kind of animal was sneaking through our camp last night.

"And it wasn't any of the ones we named.

"Take a look at this!"

He held up a pair of large horn-rimmed glasses.

He said, "The animal was a HUMAN! And we better find out what that human was doing here!"

Chapter 3:
The Fight for the Park

In a few minutes they were all dressed. They washed their faces and hands in the river.

The more they thought about a person

sneaking around in the dark, the worse they felt. They hardly talked.

Quickly, they made some oatmeal for breakfast.

They were just about to eat when they heard a car coming along the road.

Sammy jumped up. He yelled, "Look, it's Dr. Luke!"

They all waved as Dr. Justin Luke drove in with his old beat-up green camper.

He wasn't a medical doctor. He studied fossils, mostly dinosaur fossils.

The canyon was his special place.

One day, ten years ago, he had gone climbing up the canyon wall. He reached a rock ledge partway up.

He took one look. He couldn't believe it! The ledge was covered with footprints.

Dr. Luke was looking at tracks left millions of years before by dinosaurs.

After that, he and some of his college students dug into other rocks all over the canyon. They found more fossils ... most of a dinosaur skeleton and seven dinosaur eggs.

Now Dr. Luke got out of his camper and hugged them all.

Sammy began to giggle when Dr. Luke hugged Mrs. Tandy.

He poked Bill. He said, "Mrs. T.'s got another boyfriend."

Mrs. Tandy said, "Sammy, why don't

you go eat your oatmeal!"

Bill said, "And I'll get some for the professor."

They all sat down and told Dr. Luke about finding the horn-rimmed glasses.

He looked very worried. He said, "That's just what I was afraid of. I have a story to tell you. It should explain why I invited you here.

"This last year I've been in a race to save this canyon."

Dave asked, "What do you mean? I thought you said they were going to make it a national park."

Dr. Luke said, "They're supposed to, this year. The land is supposed to be set aside for fossil study and camping.

"But some people are trying to keep it from being a park.

"And they've been trying to scare us away all year."

Kathy said, "But who would want this land? It's so dry ... too dry to grow things ... and I bet there are snakes!"

Sammy said, "Yeah! Who? If I get my hands on them, I'll ... "

Dr. Luke smiled. "I can't say who, for sure, because I don't have final proof. But I have a good idea."

Dave said, "Well, what did they do to try to scare you off?"

Dr. Luke said, "Once they sneaked into camp when we were gone, and stole our stove.

"They've cut big holes in our tents ... twice! And once they took all our food.

"There were twenty-four students working here with me. We had to drive a hundred miles to get enough food to replace what they stole."

Mrs. Tandy said, "They sound like monsters!"

Dr. Luke said, "That's not the worst of it. We've heard gun shots near our camp a few times.

"And once, at night, they dropped big rocks near our campsite from the top of the canyon.

"But I never dreamed they would bother YOU if I wasn't here."

Bill said, "They could have killed you! Who do you THINK is doing it?"

Dr. Luke said, "Miners. There's a big mining company trying to keep the canyon from being saved as a national park.

"They've been looking here for metals to mine. And they think the canyon is full of them.

"They're trying to make the government believe there are no more fossils here.

"And, they're trying to make everyone think that the canyon is too dangerous to be a national park ... that gangs hang out here.

"And they're trying to scare me away from hunting for fossils."

Mrs. Tandy said, "How can we help you, Justin?"

Dr. Luke said, "I want you to help me prove that the canyon is safe ... prove that all these troubles are only caused by the mining company.

"And while you're here, I HAVE to find another important fossil.

"If I do, the government will make it a national park. I have their promise."

Sammy said, "Then let's go! What are we waiting for?"

Dr. Luke said, "Wait a minute, Sammy. We need to plan first. I don't want any of you to get hurt."

Dave said, "I think it's important that we stick together. And one of us should always be on the lookout for trouble. Even at night!"

Sammy said, "I wish we had some of those spy glasses that work in the dark, like the army has.

"Then if anyone tried to sneak up on us, WHAM! I'd get him!"

The others laughed.

Dr. Luke said, "You know, Sammy, I do, too. Those glasses pick up heat waves, rather than light waves. That's why they work in the dark!

"But right now, let's start digging."

Dave asked, "Are we going to start someplace that I can get to with my chair? If not, I'll stay here and keep an eye out for trouble."

Dr. Luke said, "Well, I do want you to see the ledge where we found the dinosaur eggs and the tracks.

"You can wheel along the canyon top to get to it. There's a narrow and steep path down, but it's only a few feet long.

"And the ledge is very wide. The boys can carry you easily."

He turned to Mrs. Tandy. "Becky, why don't you take Dave's chair down when we get there? Kathy and I can carry the tools.

"We can practice digging there. After that we should head down to the canyon."

Bill said, "What if the miners get into

our camping stuff?"

Dr. Luke said, "We don't need to worry about that right now. We can see our cars and our camp from the ledge. They wouldn't dare bother them."

So they set out to see the dinosaur tracks.

Chapter 4:
The Enemy Shows Up

They walked along the canyon top.

Bill pointed to a piece of blue plastic, nailed to one of the dry-looking trees.

He said, "Who in the world would do

that? Look, there's another tree with a piece of yellow plastic, and one with a red piece."

Dr. Luke said, "Uh-oh! Those markers weren't there the last time I was here.

"Looks like the miners think they've found several metals here. Each color stands for a different ore."

Sammy said, "Oar? You mean the things you paddle boats with? They found them here, on top of a canyon?"

Dr. Luke laughed. "No, O-R-E, ore, the rock that you find metals in.

"Now here we are. Here's the path that goes down to the ledge."

Sammy said, "Lucky for us these bushes are growing here. If we fall, they'll catch us!"

Step by careful step, they made their way down, carrying Dave.

Mrs. Tandy put his chair on a

flat place.

They helped Dave into it.

Then they looked around.

The ledge they stood on was wider than a living room. It ran along the canyon wall for about fifty feet.

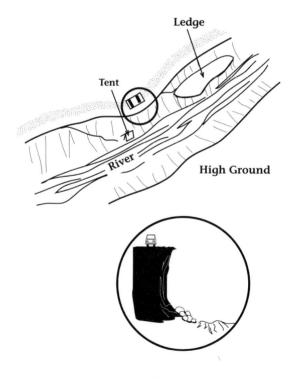

Ledge

Tent

River

High Ground

They saw dinosaur tracks all over it.

Big tracks.

Little tracks.

Tracks on top of tracks.

Tracks going in every direction.

Bill said, "Holy cats!"

Sammy said, "You mean holy dinosaurs! This must have been a dinosaur dance hall!"

Dr. Luke pointed to a big dug-out place in the wall. It was almost a cave.

He said, "That's where we found the seven dinosaur eggs. The rock up here is pretty soft.

"It fell apart when one of my students hammered it. We saw something sticking out of the piece that fell.

"When we chipped away at the thing, we found our first dinosaur egg! It had turned to hard stone!

"It was about the size of your fist.

"We found six others near it in less than an hour."

Kathy said, "It looks like some of the tracks lead right up to the wall. Why?"

Dr. Luke said, "Millions of years ago this ledge was much wider. It was a wide, muddy road for dinosaurs.

"Through the years the mud turned into hard rock, with their tracks still in it. Years after that, the ledge became covered with several feet of dust. The dust turned into soft rock."

Dave said, "I've read about how these rocks form. I bet as the years went by, wind and rain wore a lot of that soft rock away. So now we can see some dinosaur tracks again."

Dr. Luke said, "Right! Now let's practice digging more of the wall away. But be very careful not to chip any fossils."

He handed a small pick and safety

glasses to each person.

Then he broke a piece of rock out of the wall with his pick.

With great care, he broke that piece into small pieces with a little hammer.

They spent about half an hour breaking pieces out of the wall.

Then Dr. Luke said, "You've all got the hang of it. Let's head for the bone dig."

But before they gathered their tools together, Kathy heard a far-off humming sound.

She said, "What's that! I hear a noise. I think it's a plane."

The others listened.

Dave said, "It sounds like a chopper to me. Like the helicopter the Coast Guard uses back in Bluff Lake."

Dr. Luke said, "It must be the miners' helicopter. There it is, coming over those tree tops."

Sammy said, "Hey! They're heading right toward us!"

He grabbed Bill's arm and held on tight.

The helicopter came so close, it shook the air around them.

It made a terrible pounding noise.

Dave yelled, "Cover your ears!

"Stay right where you are!"

He reached out and pulled Kathy over to him.

Her thin body was shaking, but she stared right into the face of the pilot of the helicopter.

She could see him laughing, and pointing them out to the man who was sitting next to him.

The other man was laughing, too.

After another minute, the chopper flew upward and away.

Dr. Luke said, "Well, guys, now you've seen the enemy."

Bill said, "And now we have to start fighting back! Lead us down to those bones!"

Chapter 5:
Starting the Hunt

They worked their way up the path from the ledge.

They went across the canyon top, and back down to their camp.

Dave said, "Now we have a real problem. Are we going to be able to keep an eye on our camp from the dig?"

Dr. Luke shook his head. He said, "I'm sorry to tell you this, after you've gone to all the trouble of un-packing.

"But the miners might attack the camp if they see we've left.

"I wish I had told you when I invited you ... not to set up camp until I came. I didn't think you would get here before I did.

"Since we don't want to split up, that means we need to leave our stuff packed in our cars every day.

"I have a new alarm on my camper that's so loud you could hear it down the canyon for miles. The dig's around that bend about a third of a mile.

"That's about fifteen minutes away, over this rough ground."

Bill said, "Oh, well. Let's get started re-packing."

Dave said, "Just a minute. Maybe we can think of another way."

Sammy said, "We can! I know exactly what we can do!

"We can dig a pit in front of our tent. They'll fall into it if they try to mess with anything. Just like in this movie I saw!"

Bill said, "Come on, Sammy. That would take us forever. This ground is as hard as rock."

Then Kathy said, "Maybe we could tie some string to our tent and take the string ball with us around the bend. Then if anyone walks there, we will see our line move and we can go after him."

Dr. Luke said, "I'm afraid the dig is too far away for that to work."

Bill said, "Then just this once, let's

take a chance they'll leave our stuff alone. After all, it's only for one day."

The rest of them agreed.

So they followed the river down the canyon to the bone dig.

They started digging where Dr. Luke pointed.

About half an hour later, the helicopter flew high over them.

Dr. Luke said, "Don't pay attention to them. They'll be spying on us from time to time as we work."

At first they all worked hard, carefully digging out chunks of stone.

But after a while Sammy sat down with a mad look on his face.

Mrs. Tandy stopped digging. She called, "What's wrong, Sammy?"

Sammy said, "I'm SO hot, and that river looks SO cool. I know we can't, but I wish we could swim in it."

Dr. Luke said, "Why can't we? My students and I always swim in it to keep cool. But when I say cool, I mean COOL! Do you want to give it a try?"

Sammy said, "Sure, but we didn't bring our swimsuits."

Dr. Luke said, "Who said anything about swimsuits? The sun is so hot, we can go in with our clothes on.

"The wet clothes keep you cool until the sun dries them out. Then you go in again."

Sammy said, "Oh, look, here comes the chopper! I bet they wish they were down here swimming instead of up there spying!"

So Bill and Sammy carried Dave in his chair into a quiet pool a little ways down the canyon.

The others followed.

Dave lowered himself into the fast-moving water. It was really cold!

In less than a minute he was pulling himself back up into his chair.

Sammy was screaming, "Let's get out of here. I'm freezing!"

He and Bill ran over to Dave and the two of them carried him out.

Kathy, Mrs. Tandy, and Dr. Luke hurried out after them.

They went back to their hunting ground.

Kathy hit her pick into the canyon wall. Some pieces of rock flew out and hit Mrs. Tandy on the side of her face.

Kathy cried, "Oh, Mrs. T., I'm so sorry! Are you all right?"

Mrs. Tandy just laughed and said, "I'm perfectly fine. These safety glasses saved my eyes."

Still, Kathy felt bad.

To keep from hitting anybody else, she walked down the canyon.

She hit her pick into a big shelf of rock.

The whole shelf fell off and broke into pieces.

The next minute Kathy was screaming at the top of her lungs, "HEY! COME HERE! LOOK AT WHAT HAPPENED!"

Chapter 6:
Kathy's Discovery

Everyone rushed to see what had happened to Kathy.

Dave almost tipped his wheelchair over in his hurry to get to her.

He called out, "Kathy! Kathy, are you OK?"

But Kathy just kept pointing toward the ground.

Mrs. Tandy ran up to her and hugged her. She asked, "Are you hurt? Did the rock fall on your foot?"

Kathy began to laugh. "No, no, I'm not hurt. But look at that."

They all looked down.

The large rock shelf she had knocked down had split into two layers.

A piece of the top layer had flown off ... and peeking out was a pattern of some kind on the bottom layer.

Dr. Luke was down on his knees in a second.

He started lifting all the upper pieces off of the bottom pieces.

One by one, very carefully, he laid them a few feet away, still face down as they had fallen.

They all watched with their mouths open.

Finally, he took off the last piece of the top layer. There on the bottom layer of stone was a perfect, whole skeleton print.

It was the skeleton of an animal about the size of a police dog.

It had long hind legs and short front legs.

Sammy took one look and said, "What is that? A kangaroo with big teeth?"

Dr. Luke said, "I don't know! I can't wait till I get back to the camper and bring my books down here."

Dave asked, "It sure looks like a Tyrannosaurus rex, but I always thought they were huge."

Mrs. Tandy said, "Now come on, Justin. You know more about dinosaurs than almost any person on earth! Can't you tell us what this thing is?"

In a slow, quiet, mysterious voice, Dr. Luke said, "I may be dreaming, but I don't think I've ever seen this skeleton before.

"And I can't remember it from any photos.

"I can only remember it in charts and drawings.

"I think I can safely say that Kathy has found the most important fossil in this whole canyon.

"If I'm right, this is an older type of dinosaur than anyone has ever seen before. We've all hoped it would be found someday."

The next minute, careful Dr. Luke yelled, "YAHOO!"

He grabbed Kathy up in his arms and danced in a circle with her in the air.

Then he put her down and grabbed Mrs. Tandy and did a dance with her!

Sammy, of course, giggled.

At last Dr. Luke calmed down.

Bill said, "So what do we do next? Do we move the fossil back to the camp?"

Dr. Luke said, "No, that's risky. We might break the pieces even more. We have to leave it here for now.

"I need to get back to my camper, though. I need my cameras. I'll have to photograph it.

"Then we can lay it out on a board. We can carry it out in a few days, after we get some people to help us."

Dave said, "I'll stay here till you get back."

Kathy said, "Then I'll stay with Dave."

The others ran back and got the things Dr. Luke needed.

They brought ...

cameras

film

plastic padding

tripods

lights

notebooks

a big plywood board

... and books on dinosaurs.

Dr. Luke took pictures of the skeleton print from every side.

Then they moved the pieces of the bottom layer onto the plywood board.

The pieces fit together like a jig-saw puzzle.

Dr. Luke took more pictures.

He patted the cameras as he hung them back around his neck.

He said, "These have become good friends. I even have a little darkroom in my camper, to print the pictures."

By that time it was 2:30.

Suddenly Sammy yelled, "Hey, I'm starved!"

Mrs. Tandy said, "Thank goodness someone remembered lunch. I'm starved, too."

She picked up her big bag and pulled out ...

a bottle of water

paper cups

dill pickles

a giant-sized box of potato chips

a box of golden raisins

bread

peanut butter and jelly

... and the biggest surprise of all, oatmeal cookies.

Sammy said, "Hey! When did you make those?"

Mrs. Tandy said, "Bill and I made them before we left home. I took them out in honor of Kathy's dinosaur."

Sammy said, "Where did you hide them in the van?"

Mrs. Tandy said, "I'm not telling."

Bill said, "Pass me those cups, and I'll pour the water. Give me a hand, Sammy."

But Sammy was already munching on a sandwich.

So Kathy helped Bill.

In fifteen minutes they were eating the last cookies when Bill said, "Oh my gosh! Listen."

Kathy said, "What? I don't hear anything."

Bill said, "I think I heard a car motor. In the direction of our camp. I bet somebody is messing around there!"

Chapter 7:
Bill's Discovery

They jumped up and started for their camp, fast. Ten minutes later, they ran around the bend.

What a mess!

Boxes of food were spilled all over.

Sleeping bags were thrown everywhere.

The tent was knocked down.

Kathy said, "Oh, no! Now what do we do?"

But Mrs. Tandy said, "I know exactly what we do.

"We pick up all our things and set up our tent again.

"Then tomorrow morning we pack it all into the van. We aren't going to let those rats scare us off."

Sammy shouted, "Hooray, Mrs. T.!" and hugged her.

Dr. Luke said, "I'm really sorry about this, guys. But if you can clean up the mess without me, I'll get busy in my darkroom."

They started cleaning up.

Bill said, "Yikes! A lot of these food cans are dented."

Kathy said, "I looked them over, though. They're OK. We can use up the ones that are in the worst shape for dinner tonight."

Two hours later they were finished. They knocked on Dr. Luke's camper.

He opened the door right away.

He had a package under his arm.

He said, "I've decided to drive to the U.S. Air Force base, about twenty-five miles away.

"I can report the attack on our camp to the sheriff, on their radio.

"And I can give them my photos to mail to the college.

"You must all promise to stay close together, and near the van, to be safe."

Dave said, "We will be just fine."

Mrs. Tandy said, "And when you get back, we can promise you a VERY interesting dinner!"

After Dr. Luke left, Sammy said, "What's for dinner that's so interesting?"

Kathy pointed to four badly dented cans. She said, "We should use these up tonight because they might have tiny holes in them."

Sammy read their labels aloud.

"Cream of shrimp soup.

"Sardines.

"Tuna.

"Salmon."

Then he said, "Hmm ... there's something fishy about this dinner."

Kathy groaned. She said, "I knew SOMEone was going to say that!"

Bill mixed some bread in with the fish.

When Dr. Luke got back, Mrs. Tandy said, "Time to eat."

Dr. Luke looked inside the bowl. He said, "I'll eat it, but what is it?"

Sammy said, "Fish mush!"

Everybody LOVED it!

Then Dave said, "It's still light out. Are we going to work on the dinosaur rocks tonight?"

Dr. Luke said, "No, I want to do some reading before I study them. So I'll have some ideas to give the newspapers about Kathy's dino bones."

Kathy said, "The NEWSPAPERS!"

Dr. Luke said, "People all around the

world will want to visit this canyon.

"If we let everyone know about it, the government will HAVE to turn this place into a park. Besides, they promised they would."

Sammy said, "Well, if we aren't working on the skeleton, I have something to do!"

He ran to the van. In five minutes he came out in plastic wading pants that came up as high as his armpits.

He was holding a fishing pole.

Bill said, "You little rat! I thought we decided we didn't have room! So I left mine at home!"

Sammy said, "Mrs. T. isn't the only one with hiding places in the van. I even brought YOUR poles and waders, too. I'll tell you where they are ... for a nickel."

He turned and ran.

Kathy and Bill ran after him.

He ran straight into the fast-moving river, up to his knees.

He cast out his line.

In a minute he yelled, "Oops! The rubber worm is stuck on something underwater."

He reached down.

He couldn't feel the worm, so he bent down even more.

Suddenly, cold water poured into the top of his waders.

He yelled, "Yow! What happened? Hey! Something's got me!"

He waved his arms wildly as the water pulled him down river in his heavy, water-filled pants.

In a minute Bill and Kathy were racing down the riverbank.

Then they pushed their way through the fast-moving water to reach him.

They pulled him back to dry land.

They helped him out of his waders.

When they turned them upside-down, about a gallon of water spilled out.

Sammy hated for anyone to think he was scared, so he said, "Well, THAT was a nice little water ride!"

Then he added, "I forgot to take off my watch. Why didn't you remind me, Bill?"

Bill said, "You pest. We should have let you float away."

Sammy waved his fishing pole and

said, "At least I didn't lose this. I'm going to catch a fish, but from the bank, not wading."

Kathy shook her head and said, "I don't even want to watch this. See you back at the camp!"

But Bill said, "I'm staying with you, Sammy. I'm not going to let you float away even if you are a goofball."

He sat down against a rock on the bank.

He picked up a stone.

He took one look at it. Suddenly he was shouting, "COME ON, SAMMY! QUICK!"

He went running back to camp, yelling and waving the stone in the air.

Chapter 8:
Dinosaur Thieves

When Dr. Luke saw Bill's stone, his mouth opened ... but no words came out.

Slowly he reached out and took the stone.

He held it gently in both hands.

Bill said, "Is it what I think it is?"

At last Dr. Luke said, "It sure is, Bill. You've found a dinosaur egg!

"I can't believe it. I've been searching here for ten years, and in one day you kids have made two great finds.

"But where WAS this egg, Bill? Can you take me to the exact spot?"

Bill said, "Sure. At least I think so. I guess I was so excited about finding it, I didn't notice exactly where I was."

Sammy said, "Don't worry, I know where I was. You can figure out where

you were from that.

"I was standing on a big red rock that stuck out into the river. There were two big twisted poplar trees near it, one on each side."

Sammy, Bill, and Dr. Luke began to look for the rock, but there were a LOT of big red ones.

And there were a lot of poplar trees, too.

Finally Sammy said, "There's the right rock. I remember looking across the river when I was standing on it.

"I noticed that big crack in the canyon wall, straight across on the other side."

Bill said, "He's right. And there's the rock I was leaning against when I found the egg."

Dr. Luke looked at the ground. He said, "This isn't the kind of place where I'd expect to find this kind of dinosaur egg.

"And anyway, it's rare to find just one egg. They're laid in nests, several eggs together."

By then Dave and the others had arrived.

Dave said, "Could the stone egg have been carried to this spot by the river? Or could it have fallen from higher up?"

They all looked up at the cliff in back of them. Then they looked higher and higher until they all saw the same thing at once.

Far above them was the ledge ... the ledge with the dinosaur nest on it!

Kathy asked, "So do you think this might have washed down here years ago from that nest of eggs up there?"

Dr. Luke said, "Well, that would make sense ... except that we are about thirty feet up-river from that nest."

Dave said, "Well, let's look around. Maybe there are other eggs around, no matter how they got here."

They all began searching the ground around them.

At last Dr. Luke said, "I should get back to the camper. It will be light for another few hours.

"I want to look through my books for Kathy's dinosaur, and give Bill's egg some thought."

Dave said, "We have some books on dinosaurs we want to read, too."

71

But just half an hour later they heard a motor beating through the air again.

They saw the helicopter coming through the canyon.

It flew above their camp and circled low around them, slowly.

Bill said, "You know, they must be counting us or something."

Then, very suddenly, the helicopter darted away.

To their surprise, it looked like it was going to land in the canyon.

Dr. Luke said, "That's strange. They've never risked a landing between the canyon walls. The winds are very tricky in there for a helicopter.

"I wonder what they're up to."

Then suddenly he yelled, "Kathy's DINOSAUR!"

Dave yelled, "Go on. Run! I'll follow as fast as I can!"

72

Kathy stayed with Dave. The others raced over rocks and roots and branches.

They tripped and slid.

Dr. Luke yelled as he ran, "How could they know we found something important?"

Mrs. Tandy gasped, "What could they do to it?"

Sammy yelled, "Just wait till you see what I do to THEM!"

But Sammy didn't get that chance.

Before they got to the dinosaur dig, they heard the helicopter take off.

They saw it rise slowly in the air and fly away.

Five minutes later, at last, they ran around the bend to the dig.

The plywood board was there.

But it was bare.

The stones they had put on it were gone.

Chapter 9:
The Night Raid!

Sammy said, "Those chicken-faced rat-pigs!"

Mrs. Tandy said, "I can't believe anyone would do this!"

Dr. Luke said, "Some people let NOTH-
ING stand in the way of making money!

"I don't even know if the head of the
mining company knows what these guys
are doing. They're trying to force us to
give up."

Mrs. Tandy said, "I wonder how they
knew about the skeleton?"

Dr. Luke said, "Maybe one of them
knows someone at the Air Force base."

Sammy said, "Why don't we just tell
the police?"

Bill said, "If we do, how can we prove
they were the ones who stole it?"

Dr. Luke said, "That's just it. We
have to catch them in the act."

Bill said, "Well, Sammy and I will go
back and tell Dave and Kathy. Come
on, Sammy."

When Dave saw the looks on their
faces, he called, "How bad is it, guys?"

Bill said, "The worst! The men in the helicopter took Kathy's dinosaur from the board."

Kathy said sadly, "Poor Dr. Luke. We feel terrible, but it must be even worse for him."

Sammy said, "Hmm ... that's weird. He seemed mad. But he didn't seem that upset."

Dave said, "Then things may not be as bad as you think."

In a few minutes, they got back to the dinosaur dig.

Dave said, "I heard those crooks took the fossil, Dr. Luke. Did they take the top layer, too?"

Dr. Luke smiled. "No, thank goodness. We still have it! And my pictures, too."

Sammy said, "I don't see what good the top of the shelf would do us. Just a bunch of bare rock!"

But Kathy said, "Oh, I see. It ISN'T just bare rock!"

Dr. Luke turned one of the pieces over. He said, "Nope. Look at this!"

Sammy said, "Hey! It's the dinosaur skeleton! How did it get there?"

Dave said, "The top and bottom layers made a sandwich, with the skeleton pressed in between. We still have the top print."

Sammy said, "Well, those rotten clowns aren't getting their hands on IT! Dr. Luke, we have to get it back to your camper, right now!"

Kathy said, "But how can we get all these stones back? They're so heavy."

Bill said, "Maybe we could pull them on the board, like a sled."

Dr. Luke said, "Great idea! All we have to do is figure out a way to drag it."

Kathy said, "Well, we could use rope, but how would we fasten it to the board?"

Then Mrs. Tandy said, "When I was a little girl, my father drilled a hole in a board so he could pull me on it.

"But I don't suppose we could pull the stones that way. The rope would wear out."

Dr. Luke said, "Not if we made wooden runners, to keep the board off the ground."

Dave said, "Why don't you and Sammy go get what we need to do it? The rest of us can guard the stones until you get back."

Dr. Luke said, "We need a suitcase, too, for the small pieces. And towels to wrap the rocks."

In an hour, they had the sled ready.

The ones who didn't pull the sled pushed Dave. He held the suitcase across his wheelchair.

It took them over an hour to get back to camp.

Sammy said, "We made it! And I could have pulled it twice as far!"

He beat his chest with his fists. He said, "I'm as strong as a moose!"

Bill said, "You look like one, too. Now go sit down. You did most of the pulling."

Sammy wiped the sweat from his face with his shirt. He said, "Not me. Let's go. What do we do next?"

They put all the fossils inside the camper.

Dr. Luke said, "Now you folks get comfortable in your tent. I'm going to be working, so I'll keep watch until I get tired."

It was the middle of the night.

The Woodlanders were all asleep.

Suddenly Dave felt someone shaking him.

He heard Dr. Luke whisper, "Wake up. Keep quiet. Help me wake the others.

You've got to get out of this tent!"

They woke everybody up.

Dr. Luke whispered, "Kathy and Becky, grab the wheelchair. We can't let anything happen to that.

"Sammy and Bill, we three can carry Dave. We've got to get away in a hurry. And keep as quiet as you can.

"I heard someone moving around on the cliff right above us.

"There's no telling what's going to happen next!"

Chapter 10:
The Attack

In the dark, they headed toward the river. They ducked behind some bushes.

And not a moment too soon.

They heard a clatter of rocks landing

near their tent.

Kathy said, "I feel like a rabbit hiding from a dog ... listening to see if it's going to get me."

Another rock fell.

Another.

More.

Then Sammy whispered, "Hey, what happened? The rocks stopped."

They all listened. Nothing.

Then they heard someone running through the bushes on the top of the cliff.

Sammy grabbed hold of Bill's arm.

Then they heard men's voices.

"Oof!"

"Oh!"

"Ow-w-w-w!"

Then someone called, "Run, Don, run for the jeep!"

They heard a motor start, and a car drive away.

Bill said, "Let's get our flashlights and see what shape our tent is in."

Dave said, "Then let's head up to the cliff."

To their surprise, the tent was all right.

Sammy said, "Man, they're no sharpshooters! They completely missed it! It's probably because that guy lost his glasses when he was snooping around here. Serves him right!"

They took their flashlights and started up to the top of the canyon.

It was so dark, they took it slow. They had to pick their way around the sage bushes.

Finally, they were above their camp.

They shined their lights all around.

Dave said, "Look at that!" He pointed to a sage bush with a broken branch.

Sammy said, "Someone must have stepped on it."

Bill said, "Or even fallen on it. This sage is pretty tough. You can't break it off that easily."

Mrs. Tandy said, "My goodness! Look over here!"

She pointed to a place where a whole bush was flattened.

Sammy walked over to the spot. He shined his light around.

Bill saw an object shining on the ground.

He ran over and picked it up. He said, "Hey! Look what I've got!"

Sammy said, "Whatever it is, it's mine. You only saw it because of MY flashlight. Give it to me!"

He tried to grab it from Bill, but Bill held him off with one arm.

In Bill's hand was a button made of silver. It was about the size of a nickel, but thinner.

Mrs. Tandy said, "Why, it's beautiful!"

Kathy said, "I wonder where it came from."

Sammy said, "Hey, it looks like it's off a dress or something. Do you think it was a woman up here who chased those men away?"

Mrs. Tandy said, "Maybe. If I had seen people throwing rocks at our tent, I'd have run after them. Maybe I'd have used that stick right there."

She picked up a thick stick.

Dave shined his light on it and said, "Hey, look at the end!"

There was a dark red stain on the very end of the stick.

He said, "I think someone DID use this to chase those men away. I think someone got hit, and that's BLOOD!"

They all crowded around to get a better look.

But Dr. Luke was still looking at the button.

Then he said, "Wait a minute. This is an American Indian design on the button. I've seen buttons like this before!"

Bill said, "There are Native Americans around here?"

Dr. Luke said, "Yep. Mostly Navajo Indians." He said the word like this: NAHV-uh-ho.

"Some of them raise sheep here. The sheep graze all over this land. Anywhere they can find a few blades of grass."

Dave said, "This Navajo chased more

than sheep. I wish we could find him, and thank him."

Dr. Luke laughed. "Good luck, but you won't find him unless he wants you to.

"If this was a sheep-herder, you can bet he knows this land better than anyone else.

"The cinder hills, the petrified forest—"

Sammy said, "Pet-re-fried forest! What do you mean? Who would ever take a pet forest and re-fry it? You re-fry beans, not pets."

Dr. Luke laughed. "No, no, not pet-re-fried. Pet-ri-FIED. That means turned to stone, turned into a fossil."

89

Sammy said, "You mean there's a whole forest of fossil trees standing around? How come I didn't see it?"

Dave said, "It's not like a forest anymore, Sammy. The trees were alive millions of years ago.

"Now they've fallen, and are lying around on the ground. They look like they're made of stone. PETROS is the Greek word for stone. That's why they call it petrified wood."

Sammy said, "Oh, STONE-I-FIED. I get it. Can we go see it, Dr. Luke?"

Dr. Luke said, "Why not? But let's get some sleep now. Those men won't try anything again tonight. They sounded pretty scared.

"We can go see the petrified forest first thing tomorrow."

Chapter 11:
Sammy's Missing

Sammy woke up before the others.

He crawled toward the tent flap on his hands and knees.

His plan was to get some cold water

in a paper cup to drip onto Bill's nose.

Quiet as a worm, he slid through the tent opening.

"YIKES!" Sammy's voice rang down the canyon. Like a shot, he backed into the tent.

Everybody woke up.

Bill cried, "Holy cow! What was that?"

Dave said, "What's wrong? You OK, guys?"

Mrs. Tandy said, "My lands!"

Kathy almost jumped through the tent.

Sammy said, "There's a man right outside our tent. He's just sitting there."

Bill went over to the tent flap. He said, "Stop trying to scare us, Sammy. It's too early in the morning."

Then he went through the flap.

They heard Bill say, "HEY! Who are you? What are you doing here!"

The rest piled out of the tent.

Kathy helped Dave into his wheelchair.

The man stood up and smiled.

He had straight, long black hair.

He wore blue jeans, and his shirt was trimmed with silver buttons.

He said, "Hi! I'm glad you're finally up. I'm John Yazzie. I raise sheep around here."

Right away Sammy hit Bill.

He whispered, "Look! His second-from-the-top button is missing!"

Just then Dr. Luke walked out of his camper.

He took a good look at the man.

He said, "Hello there! I'm Justin Luke."

Then he reached into his pocket. He pulled out a silver button and held it toward the man's shirt.

It matched the other buttons perfectly.

Dr. Luke said, "I believe this is yours," and gave it to him.

Sammy blurted out, "Then you're the guy who whacked those rats with a stick last night!"

Then he walked around in back of the man and said, "Wow! Your hair is REALLY long!"

Bill grabbed him and yanked him back. Kathy poked him.

But Sammy just pulled away and kept talking.

He said, "I love your buttons. They're beautiful."

The man smiled. He said, "Hi! What's your name?"

Sammy said, "I'm Sammy. And that's Kathy and Bill and Dave and Mrs. Tandy. And we are on a great dinosaur hunt!"

John Yazzie smiled. He said, "I figured that's what you guys were up to. Anyway, it looks like the miners aren't too happy to see you."

He pointed down the canyon.

He said, "Three miles away, two of them are camping, behind some rocks, by a cinder hill.

"They hunt for metals every day.

"Sometimes they get in their cars and chase my sheep. The running kills them.

"Those men have no respect for this land.

"We need this free grazing land for our sheep, so we watch these guys when we can.

"That's why I went up to the cliff last night."

Kathy said, "Lucky for us you did."

Mrs. Tandy said, "My, yes! Thank you! But we found a stick with blood on it. What happened? Who got hurt?"

John said, "One of those guys didn't like me getting in his way. So he came after me. I had the stick, but he didn't see it I guess. He ended up running himself into it."

Sammy said, "Hey! It's probably the guy who dropped his stupid glasses in our camp!"

John said, "So ... they really are spying on you, aren't they? Did you say

you were on a dinosaur hunt?"

Dr. Luke said, "We are trying to get this canyon made into a national park. Then it could be used for grazing.

"We've found some important dinosaur fossils.   But some of them have been stolen.

"We hope we can find more of them at the top of the canyon.   Then the government will save the upper land, too."

John Yazzie said, "I sure thank you for trying.   But be careful, OK?

"Well, I have to be going. Watch your step, now."

They all waved as he walked toward the canyon top.

Sammy whispered to the others, "Wow! I sort of feel better knowing he's around here ... keeping an eye on those creepy miners."

Mrs. Tandy nodded. "Me, too! Well, Justin, now that we are all wide awake, we might as well start digging again."

Dr. Luke said, "I suppose we better put off going to the petrified forest. It looks like the miners are desperate. What if they try to break into my camper?

"Let's stay around here. We can check out the top of the canyon wall for fossils."

Sammy said, "I think we should go over to the mining camp and tell those guys they better leave us alone!"

Dave said, "You know they'd laugh in

our faces."

Bill said, "Think about it, Sammy. Those men would love to hurt us. Don't be a drip!"

Now Sammy got MAD! He said, "If I'm a drip, you're a whole puddle!"

Dr. Luke said, "Come on. Let's get the tools and get started."

Dave said, "If you don't mind, I'd like to do some more work on the big ledge."

Dr. Luke said, "No problem. We can take you there and start up above you. You'll probably just find more dinosaur tracks. But you can keep an eye on our camp from the ledge."

A half hour later, they were all out of sight of each other, hidden by rocks.

The sounds of their picks and hammers carried along the canyon top. The sun blazed hot in the sky.

In another half hour, Bill started to

wonder where Sammy was.

He called out, "Sammy! Sammy! Where are you?"

Just then, Dave shouted out, "Hey, everyone, check this out!"

But at the same time, Kathy yelled, "HELP! Quick! Everybody, come here!"

Bill, Mrs. Tandy, and Dr. Luke ran along the cliff top and found her.

She said, "Sammy stopped by almost an hour ago. Just now I sat down to rest near my backpack.

"Look what I found sticking out of it."

It was a note from Sammy.

I'll be back in a few hours.
Bill will see who the drip is. He is!

They heard Dave call from the far-off ledge, "Is anything wrong?"

Bill shouted, "You bet there is! I think Sammy's gone to the mining camp alone!"

They ran to the ledge to show Dave Sammy's note.

Chapter 12:
Caught Red-Handed

They left their tools lying on the ground
where they had been digging.

Suddenly Bill remembered something.
He said to Dave, "Didn't I hear you call

out at the same time Kathy shouted? What was it?"

Dave said, "It can wait! Just get me off this ledge and let's go find Sammy!"

In five minutes they were all in the camper, headed down river along the canyon top.

Dr. Luke had to drive slowly. There were rocks and bushes all around.

The old camper was built to travel over rough ground. Just the same, they bumped and bounced.

About three miles along, Bill shouted, "What's going on there? Look at that!"

They all stared.

104

There was a big black hill ahead.

In front of it were a helicopter, a trailer, a jeep, and a police car.

Two men were loading a pile of rocks, one by one, into the jeep.

One of them had a big bandage wrapped around his arm.

Standing near them, arms crossed, watching quietly, stood four people. One of them was John Yazzie.

Two others were police officers.

And the fourth was Sammy, dirty as a mud ball.

Dr. Luke stopped his camper.

Sammy ran over to them.

He was a mess!

He was hot and sweaty.

He had black dust all over his clothes.

His hair was wild.

He had dried blood on his nose.

He had black rings of dirt around his

eyes, where sweat hadn't washed the dirt away.

He looked like a raccoon.

Mrs. Tandy jumped out of the camper and hugged him.

Sammy said, "Mrs. T.! Watch out for your white shirt! I'm a little dirty."

Mrs. Tandy said, "Who cares? Are you all right?"

By then they all were hugging him.

Sammy called, "Let me up for air!

I'm OK. Don't you think I can take care of myself?"

With that, the police officers and John Yazzie laughed out loud.

One of the officers walked over to the Woodlanders. She said, "Hello! I'm Sheriff Stone."

Dr. Luke said, "I'm Justin Luke, and these are the Woodlanders, my friends."

The sheriff shook hands with them.

She said, "Looks like we've got a case here against these men. And it's all because of John Yazzie's quick thinking.

"He told me this morning about the stolen fossils and the attack on your tent.

"He and I came over to the miners' camp with another officer to ask some questions.

"But while we were talking, John heard a funny noise coming from the trailer.

"He looked inside and found this

107

young fellow ... tied up ... yelling like a hoot owl ... and kicking on the door."

Sammy grinned a little. He said, "Well, I can take care of myself MOST of the time. But this was a little too hard, even for me, Sammy Westburg, the great dinosaur rock spy."

Bill said, "I can't believe this. What have you done now, Sammy?"

Sammy said, "Well, I was chipping away above the canyon. And I was thinking about how the miners spied on us, and threw rocks at our tent.

"And I was thinking about how nobody thought my idea of talking to the miners was any good.

"I got mad.

"Then I got madder.

"And finally, when I got the maddest, I threw down my pick and moved into action!"

Bill said, "Sammy, those miners could have really hurt you!"

Sammy said, "I thought a lot while I was walking here. I decided you were right ... that trying to talk to them would be stupid.

"So I decided to spy on them, like they've been doing on us.

"When I got near them, I hid behind some rocks and bushes.

"I worked my way around in back of that weird hill behind their camp.

"Then I started to climb up it.

"It was hard work, too. Every time you take a step, you slide back a little.

"When I got partway up, I sneaked around toward their side.

"Just when I got to where I could watch them, my foot slipped.

"The next thing I knew, I was rolling and sliding and bouncing down through

109

some black stuff.

"What IS that, anyway?"

Dr. Luke said, "Those are cinders. Millions of years ago there used to be volcanos around here.

"We think they sometimes shot cinders out ... so many that they made those hills."

Mrs. Tandy said, "Sammy, it's a wonder you didn't break a leg! Are you sure you're OK, honey?"

Sammy said, "Sure. I'm strong. You should've seen how hard they had to work to get me into their trailer.

"Anyway, when Sheriff Stone let me out, I saw a bunch of rocks all dumped in a pile. They were Kathy's dinosaur fossils!

"The sheriff said she would bring them to you in the jeep before she takes the men to jail."

Sheriff Stone said, "And I will! We need to keep those fossils safe!"

Dave said, "And do I have something to show all of you!"

Chapter 13:
Dave's Discovery

Back at the camp, the police officer guarded the miners.

Sheriff Stone and the others un-loaded the fossils.

Then Dave said, "Over to the ledge, everybody. You've got to see this. If you can take those guys to jail later, Sheriff Stone, I want you to see this, too.

"After all, you and John saved Sammy!"

Sheriff Stone said, "No problem! They'll get to jail soon enough."

One of the miners said, "You don't have any reason to take us to jail. You'd better let us go."

Sheriff Stone said, "Sure. No reason at all. Just stealing, and throwing rocks. And wait till the judge hears about your kidnapping a poor little child!"

One of the miners said, "SOME POOR LITTLE CHILD! He's a monster! Before we got him into the trailer, he kicked me in both shins.

"He bit my partner on the arm. You can see the blood on his sleeve."

114

The other one said, "He's a brat!"

Bill hugged Sammy, and said, "One of the best!"

Sammy just grinned.

They climbed along the canyon top and down to the ledge.

At the far end ... up-river from the first nest ... Dave showed them a new place where he had been digging.

Dr. Luke said, "No! I don't believe my eyes!"

There, sticking out of the stone, was a dinosaur egg. Another egg was sticking out near the middle of the ledge.

Dave said, "I just KNEW Bill's dinosaur egg had washed down from the ledge, too.

"I bet there are a lot of nests up here, all over it. Not just one."

Dr. Luke began pounding Dave on the back.

Then he grabbed everyone and hugged and pounded them.

He said, "Do you know what this means? This is the first discovery of these dinosaurs nesting near each other.

"This is going to save the upper land for sure.

"The whole area will be made into a park!

"Another great discovery!"

He began dancing around on the ledge.

Kathy said, "Hold on, there. Wait a

minute! Let's get away from here before you dance right off!"

Dr. Luke said, "I've got to get to a telephone and call the newspapers. There will be reporters swarming all over here two hours after I call.

"And, I have to call the park office to send guards."

Sheriff Stone said, "Well, I've got to get those two guys to jail. I'll be back to ask Sammy and the rest of you some questions in a couple of hours."

Sammy said, "And we've got to get down, too. In a hurry!"

117

They went back to the camp.

Sheriff Stone left with the miners.

John Yazzie left to check on his sheep.

Finally the dinosaur hunters were alone.

Kathy turned to Sammy. She said, "Why did you say you were in a hurry, too?"

Sammy said, "Because we only have two hours before everyone gets back here.

"Quick, Mrs. Tandy! Get the rest of the oatmeal cookies into the van. And plastic cups and water.

"First we drive over to make your phone calls, Dr. Luke.

"Then, Stonified Woods, here we come!"

So, laughing and munching, Dr. Luke and the Woodlanders piled into the van and drove off toward the petrified forest.